THIS BOOK BELONGS TO

First published in hardback in the United Kingdom by HarperCollins *Children's Books* in 2022
HarperCollins *Children's Books* is a division of HarperCollins*Publishers* Ltd
1 London Bridge Street, London SE1 9GF

www.harpercollins.co.uk

HarperCollins*Publishers*
1st Floor, Watermarque Building, Ringsend Road, Dublin 4, Ireland

1 3 5 7 9 10 8 6 4 2

Text by Alison Sage
Text copyright © HarperCollins*Publishers* Ltd 2022
Illustrations copyright © Sarah Gibb 2022

ISBN: 978-0-00-851400-6

Printed in Italy

HarperCollins *Children's Books*

SNOW WHITE

SARAH GIBB

any years ago, there was a king and a queen who ruled a little woodland kingdom.

On the coldest, darkest day in winter, the queen found she was going to have a baby, and when a little girl was born in spring she and the king were so happy they couldn't stop smiling and laughing. Everyone came to see the new princess, even the deer and rabbits from the forest and the robins and sparrows from the fields.

The little princess grew up as beautiful as she was kind and clever. Her dark hair was curly and wild, and her eyes were as huge and dark as woodland pools.

She had a long and very grand name, which began: Her Royal Highness Priscilla Victoria Ursula Beatrice Esmeralda . . . but everyone simply called her Snow White. She was never happier than when she could play among the trees with her friends.

The king and queen's happiness didn't last. The queen fell ill and although the doctors did everything they could, she died in the king's arms. "Look after our Snow White . . ." she whispered.

The king was so unhappy he shut himself away for many months, until one day a new princess came to visit him from a distant kingdom. She was hoping to make the king fall in love with her.

This princess was dazzlingly beautiful, but she was also cruel and cunning. She pretended to be loving, but she didn't care about anyone but herself. The king only saw her beauty, and in time he asked her to marry him. Soon, everyone else saw how heartless their new queen could be. They might have been even more worried if they had seen what was hidden in her room. It was a mirror that told her anything she wanted to know.

The new queen loved to stand in front of it and ask, "Mirror, mirror, on the wall, who is the most beautiful of all?"

And the mirror would answer, "Beauty comes and beauty goes, but you are the loveliest as everyone knows."

And then the queen would smile and be almost pleasant – for an hour or two.

Years passed and the queen took no notice of Snow White, though she took care to keep her stepdaughter away from the king.

Snow White never had new clothes and wasn't allowed to go to palace parties. She ate her supper in the kitchen with the cooks and the cleaners. But everyone loved her dearly because she was as happy as a singing bird and she grew lovelier and kinder each day.

One morning, everything changed. The queen saw Snow White playing outside, and she overheard a gardener say, "My! Isn't the young princess lovely!"

A terrible thought crossed the queen's mind. She ran up to her room and cried, "Mirror, mirror, on the wall, who is the most beautiful of all?"

The mirror sang out, "My queen, you are beautiful, it's true, but young Snow White is lovelier than you!"

The queen burned with rage and jealousy. How could she get rid of Snow White for ever? The answer seemed simple. She would order one of the huntsmen to take the girl deep into the forest and lose her. She would never find her way back home.

The young huntsman was far too scared to disobey the queen. He led Snow White into the darkest, thickest part of the forest, where the trees grew so closely together they could hardly force their way through. Snow White loved the forest and was never happier than when she could explore, but she was suddenly

afraid of the huntsman's sad face.

"What's the matter?" she asked. "You're crying!"

"You must run away," he said, "far from the queen
until you are safe!"

And he stumbled off, leaving her all alone.

Snow White was not scared at first. The deer and the rabbits and the birds were her friends, and they wandered through the forest together throughout the long, sunny afternoon. But it began to get dark, and the deer drifted away. She was beginning to feel cold, hungry and tired when an owl appeared on great silent wings.

"I'll follow you," she cried, and soon the trees opened out into a clearing. In the middle stood a little cottage. Twinkling lights at the windows seemed to be welcoming her in.

She walked up to the small front door and bravely rang the bell.

A chorus of voices answered, and she heard the sound of bolts being dragged across as the door opened.

Snow White gasped. In front of her were seven little people.

"Hello," said the first one.

"Who are you?" chorused the others.

"I-I'm Snow White, and I'm so tired and hungry," Snow White replied, and she explained in a tumbled rush what had happened to her.

"In that case," said the first one. "Come in!"

"Come in," said the others. "Come in!"

Snow White walked into the prettiest, tiniest home she had ever seen.

"It's a bit untidy," apologised the second, "but we haven't been home long."

Snow White was given a hot supper of cheese on toast with mushrooms, and a big mug of creamy hot chocolate. She could hardly keep her eyes open! Before too long she was shown to a tiny room that looked out on the forest, and she fell fast asleep.

In the morning, the little people had a meeting with Snow White. "Listen," said the one who had spoken first. "It's such a long time since we had company ... and we could keep you safe from the queen. Will you stay?"

"Will you?" echoed the others hopefully.

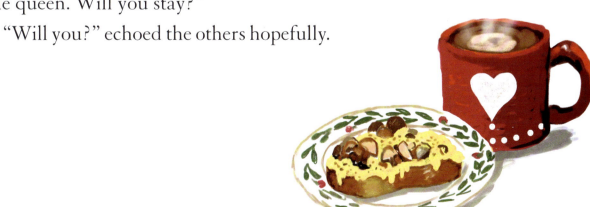

And that was how Snow White came to live in the forest. Her days were happy – playing with her animal friends and looking after the cottage while the little people were out. In the evening, they had supper and made music or played board games.

At the castle, life was not happy. The queen had asked the mirror her daily question, and it had said, "You are fine and handsome, maybe, but Snow White is lovelier, as anyone can see."

The queen shook with rage and swore that she would not sleep until Snow White was gone for ever.

First she lied to the king and told him that Snow White was an ungrateful daughter and had run away. Then she worked out a cunning plan.

She asked the mirror where Snow White was living and then she dressed up as an old woman with a basket of pretty ribbons and sashes for sale.

The queen found the little cottage in the forest and heard Snow White singing to herself.

"You won't sing for long," she muttered.

Then she called out sweetly, "Come and buy my pretty ribbons, my beautiful sashes!"

Snow White looked up and couldn't resist asking if she could try something on.

"What a pretty dress!" cooed the queen. "Let me do up this sash."

Quickly, she grabbed Snow White and pulled a sash so tight that the poor girl could not breathe and she fell down in a dead faint.

"That will teach you!" snarled the queen, and she hurried off through the forest. This time, she felt sure that Snow White was dead.

When the little people came home in the evening they were horrified to see Snow White lying still and pale. They lifted her up gently. As they did so, the first one loosened the new sash. Snow White could breathe again and the colour flooded back into her cheeks.

"That must have been the queen!" cried the little people when Snow White told them what had happened. "Never open the door to anyone while we are out!"

That evening, the queen was overcome with jealousy when the mirror told her that Snow White was still alive. She mixed a deadly potion and dipped a comb in it. Then she set off again for the forest, only this time she dressed as a young girl with a basket of combs and hair slides for sale.

At first, Snow White didn't want to open the door. But this girl looked so different from the old woman. She opened the door and the queen offered her the poisoned comb.

"Let me comb your lovely hair," she murmured. "My! It's full of tangles!" And she put the comb through Snow White's hair.

Immediately, the poison began to work and Snow White fell down as if dead.

The queen slipped away unseen, happy that her evil plan had worked.

That evening, the little people tried to find what was wrong with Snow White. Then the youngest one spotted the queen's comb, and once they had taken it out Snow White opened her eyes and smiled.

"Dear Snow White! Never, ever open the door while we are out!" they begged. "The queen has made up her mind to kill you."

The queen's anger was terrifying when the mirror told her that Snow White was still alive. This time, she chose her most deadly poison. Then she picked the sweetest-looking apple from the palace garden and put poison on to the red half. The green side she left alone. She packed her basket with fruit, dressed herself like a farm worker and set off for the cottage in the forest.

"I won't come in," she said to Snow White sweetly. "But my apples are delicious. Look! There's no danger – I'll take a bite." And she bit into the green side of the poisoned apple, which was safe.

Snow White thought to herself, *I'd love to taste that apple*. And she leaned out of her window and bit into the poisoned red side of the fruit.

Snow White tumbled to the floor as if dead, and the queen hurried away laughing. Surely Snow White could not escape this time!

The little people tried everything they could to awaken Snow White that evening, but she did not stir. How could they know that she had a piece of poisoned apple in her mouth? Weeks passed and eventually they made a crystal box, with her sad story written on it, and laid her inside. Every day they took turns to guard the box.

Many months later, a young prince lost his way in the forest and came riding by. He was amazed to see the crystal box with Snow White lying there with a little person on guard. The prince knocked at the cottage door and asked if the little people would allow him to take her away.

"I would give my kingdom to save her," he promised. "She is the only girl I could ever love."

Everyone was very upset, but they agreed that this was Snow White's best chance. Perhaps the prince would find a way to bring her back to life.

The prince was about to lift the crystal box on to his horse. But first he looked at her and tenderly gave her a kiss. As he lifted her up, the piece of poisoned apple slipped out of her mouth. Snow White's eyes fluttered and she looked up into his face.

"Where am I?" she asked.

It was hard to say who was the happiest. Was it the little people, who now had their Snow White again, or was it the prince, who had his dream princess alive in his arms? Or was it Snow White herself, who fell in love with the prince?

The prince and Snow White said a tearful goodbye to the little people, promising to come back soon. Then they set off to tell Snow White's father the joyful news that she was alive and well and about to be married. The queen was so jealous and angry to see Snow White happy that it was the worst punishment in the world for her. She fled into the forest and no one ever saw her again.

Everyone rejoiced to see their princess back home, and the celebrations began. Snow White and her prince were married and danced under the stars until dawn.

Snow White and the prince lived in great happiness together. She never forgot all her old friends, and the little people came to see them often. They loved making up games and playing with the young princes and princesses.